Once Upon A Time

Once Upon A Time

✍ Twenty Cheerful Tales to DISCARD

Read and Tell · *Selected,*

Edited and Sometimes Retold

by Rose Dobbs

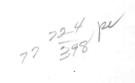

Illustrated by Flavia Gág

~~~~~~

Random House, Inc. New York

Copyrights and Acknowledgments

THANKS ARE EXTENDED to the following for permission to reprint copyrighted materi
which appears in this book: to Thomas Y. Crowell Company for "The Half Chic
from *A Treasury of Tales for Little Folks*, by Margery Bruce, copyright 1927; to T
University of Chicago Press for the adaptation of "The Lion-Makers" from *Gol
Gloom: Tales from the Panchantantra*, translated by Arthur W. Ryder, copyright 192
to Story Parade for "The Happy Cure," by Rose Dobbs, copyright 1948; to Doubleda
& Company, Inc., The Society of Authors, Miss Rose Fyleman and Messrs. Methuen
Co. Ltd. for "Why Pigs Have Curly Tails" from *The Rainbow Cat*, by Rose Fylema
copyright 1923 by Doubleday & Company; to Eva Knox Evans for "How the Milk
Way Began" from *Out Under the Sky*, copyright 1944 by Publications Committe
West Georgia College; to Harcourt, Brace and Company for "Why No One Ev
Carries the Alligator Down to the Water" from *Little Black Stories*, copyright 1929 b
Blaise Cendrars, and for "How the Letter X Got into the Alphabet," abridged fro
Rootabaga Pigeons, by Carl Sandburg, copyright 1923 by Harcourt, Brace and Compan
to Dodd, Mead and Company for "Why the Bananas Belong to the Monkey" fro
Fairy Tales from Brazil, by Elsie Spicer Eells, copyright 1917 by Dodd, Mead & Con
pany, Inc.; to G. P. Putnam's Sons and Ann Watkins, Inc. for "The Number of Spots
from *The Long Grass Whispers*, by Geraldine Elliot, copyright 1939; to Sidonie Matsn
Gruenberg for "The Three Wishes" from *Favorite Stories Old and New*, copyright 194
by Doubleday & Company, Inc.; to Coward-McCann, Inc. for "Clever Elsie" fro
Tales from Grimm, freely translated and illustrated by Wanda Gág, copyright 1936 b
Wanda Gág; to Longmans, Green and Co. for "How Many Donkeys?" from *Once th
Hodja*, copyright 1943 by Alice Geer Kelsey.

Eighth Printing

To Michael and his sister Nancy

Contents

Part I: *Ever Old, Ever New*

The Pine Tree

Retold by Rose Dobbs

In a forest grew a little pine tree. Like all other pine trees, his branches were covered with needles instead of with leaves. So he thought:

"These needles of mine do not please me. All the trees in the forest have pretty leaves. I, too, should like to have pretty leaves. But as it costs nothing to wish, and as long as I am wishing for leaves, I might as well wish for prettier leaves than the other trees have. Gold leaves! Ah, yes, how I should like to have leaves of gold!"

At night the little tree fell asleep and when he awoke in the morning, lo and behold! instead of slender green needles he found every single one of his branches covered with leaves of pure gold.

He was very happy.

"Now," he said proudly to himself, "I am more beautiful than any other tree in the whole forest. Not one of them, poor things, has such beautiful leaves as mine."

But along about noontime, a peddler with a huge sack over his shoulder wandered into the forest. The shimmering, glistening, shining, golden leaves stood out from all the rest. The peddler came up to the pine tree and, when he examined the leaves and saw that they were of pure gold, his joy knew no bounds. Quicker than it can be told, the peddler took his sack off his shoulder, put it on the ground, and went to work, stripping the pine tree of its golden leaves. Every one of them was stuffed into the huge sack, and when he had made sure that the tree was entirely bare, the peddler once more hoisted the sack and left the forest.

The pine tree shook and trembled while the golden leaves were being stripped. And now, as he shivered in the chill air, he cried:

"I shall never again ask for leaves of gold. Men will

always rob me of them. Oh, how I should like to have leaves of glass!"

At night the tree fell asleep and when he awoke in the morning, lo and behold! every one of his branches was covered with leaves of glass. The leaves of glass sparkled and shone in the sunlight. How beautiful they were! No other leaves in the forest were as beautiful as they. And our little pine tree was happy—and proud.

But along about noontime a sharp wind arose. It was a howling, growling storm wind. It whirled and swirled around the pine tree, blowing fiercely through his branches and shaking him without mercy. Every one of the glass leaves fell to the ground and broke into a thousand pieces.

Once more the pine tree was left bare, shivering in the chill air. He thought:

"Perhaps if I had ordinary green leaves, just like all the other trees in the forest, perhaps then I would be content."

At night the tree fell asleep and when he awoke in the morning, lo and behold! he was decked out in real green leaves.

But along about noontime, a frisky little goat ran into the forest and passed by the pine tree. The goat was hungry and the juicy leaves of the pine tree were just within her reach. So she ate every single one of them. And once again the pine tree found himself bare and shivering in the chill air. And now he said to himself:

"Why did I ever wish for leaves at all? What need has a pine tree for leaves? Leaves of gold, or leaves of glass, or real leaves? Someone will always steal the golden ones; the wind will throw down and shatter the glass ones; and some animal or other will be sure to eat up real leaves. Now I see that my own needles suited me best. Oh, how I wish I had them back again!"

At night the tree fell asleep and when he awoke in the morning, lo and behold! he was dressed once more in his own slender fragrant green needles.

And now at last he was really happy. And, if the truth must be told, he was lucky too—for suppose, just suppose that his last wish had not been granted!

The Half-Chick

By Margery Bruce

In the sunny land of Spain there once lived a handsome black hen. Like most hens, she was a kind and motherly bird, and very proud of her pretty yellow chicks. But once she hatched out a very queer little fellow, not the least bit like the others of the same brood. He was only half a chicken. The hen opened her beak wide, but was too startled to cluck, when he hopped out of the egg on his one leg, and waggled his one wing, and looked up at her with his one bright eye.

As he grew, the Half-chick became as mischievous and

naughty as two whole chicks rolled into one. The poor hen declared he was the most troublesome of all her many children, and got into more pranks in one day than all the others could even think of in a week. None the less, she was greatly alarmed when the Half-chick came hopping up to her on his one little leg and said:

"Mother, I have had enough of this stupid old farm. I'm off to Madrid."

"Madrid!" clucked the poor hen. "What on earth do you want to do in Madrid?"

"I want to see the King. And no doubt his Majesty will be pleased to see *me*."

"But, my poor child, have you any idea how far away Madrid is?"

"I do not care how far away it may be," returned the cheeky little Half-chick, "I'm going there, and I am going to see the King."

So off he started, hoppity-hop, in the direction where he had been told that the capital city of Spain would be found.

Presently the Half-chick came to a pretty silver brook, but its waters were choked with thick green weeds.

9

"Kind little Half-chick," said the brook, "help me, I pray you! Drag away some of these thick green weeds, so that I may run and sing once more!"

"I can't stop now," returned the Half-chick, "I'm off to Madrid to see the King."

When he had hopped a little further his way led him through a deep wood, and there he found a fire which was dying for lack of fuel.

"Amiable little Half-chick," gasped the fire, "fetch me a few sticks, or I shall die!"

"I can't stop now, I'm off to Madrid to see the King," returned the Half-chick, who was neither amiable nor kind.

By dint of long and determined hopping, the Half-chick at last reached the outskirts of Madrid, and there he saw a great chestnut-tree in full flower. The blossoming spikes of the chestnut were tossing and swaying to and fro, and from among the branches came the voice of the wind, calling for help.

"Dear little Half-chick," cried the wind, "I am tangled in this tree, and I cannot get out—do come and set me free!"

"No such thing," returned the Half-chick, unkindly. "Set *yourself* free, Sir Wind—I'm going to see the King, and I can't keep his Majesty waiting for *you.*"

Then the Half-chick hopped and hopped till he came to the palace of the King, where the tall sentinels in shining helmets and scarlet-and-yellow slashed doublets stood on guard, their great lances in their hands.

"Good," thought the conceited little Half-chick, "very good—I am expected, I see, and these fine fellows have been set here to welcome me."

So he saluted the sentinels with his one little wing as he hopped past them, and wondered why they did not return his salute.

He came to a gate in the palace wall, and, as it stood open, he slipped quickly through. Then he found himself in a dusty courtyard, and a moment later a man in a white apron and a flat white cap came out of the door of the royal kitchen.

The little Half-chick thought this must be the King himself.

"Dear me," he said, "I had no idea that a crown looked like that!"

But he drew himself up very straight on his one leg, and saluted the cook with his one little wing.

The cook looked down, and saw the queer little bird standing at his feet.

"Chicken-broth for dinner today," he remarked, cheerfully. "You are the very fellow I want, you funny Half-chick—come on!"

So he seized the Half-chick, and plumped him, just as he was, feathers and all, into the big iron pot that was bubbling on the kitchen fire.

"Oh kind water," squeaked the Half-chick, "you are hurting me—you are so hot—and so wet!"

"Have you forgotten the brook that was choked with weeds?" asked the water; and it went on bubbling and boiling faster than ever.

"Oh gentle fire," squeaked the Half-chick, "have mercy—you are hurting me, gentle fire!"

"Have you forgotten that when I asked you for mercy, you had none to spare?" retorted the fire; and it sprang up, crackling and blazing more than ever.

At that moment, there was a whistling sound in the kitchen chimney, and the Half-chick called out in despair:

"Wind, sweet Sir Wind, put out this fire, overturn this pot, and I may still escape!"

"Oh, it's you, is it?" shrilled the wind. "Well, for old acquaintance' sake, I will do my best for you!"

The Half-chick was delighted, but he soon found that the wind was speaking in jest. For it whipped him up out of the pot, and up the dark, sooty chimney, and then up, up, up, over the roofs of Madrid.

"Have you forgotten that when I was tangled in the chestnut-tree you were too much in a hurry to help me?" shouted the wind.

Higher and higher it carried the frightened Half-chick, and then, at last, it swooped down from the clouds, and planted the queer little bird on the steeple of the loftiest church-tower in Madrid.

"There you are," said the wind.

And there the Half-chick is to this day! They have painted him with gold paint, but he is very unhappy on his perch so near the clouds. Sometimes the people in the streets far below will hear a strange sound coming from the top of the steeple, and then they will say to each other, "How that weather-cock *is* creaking today!"

13

They do not know that what they take for creaking is really the mournful voice of the Half-chick, repeating again and again, "Oh, why was I not a better bird when I was young?"

The Foolish Dragon

Retold by Rose Dobbs

Long, long ago, there lived a dragon in the great China sea. More than anything else in the world this dragon loved his wife. And he spent all his time granting her every wish.

One day he noticed that his wife was not looking well. "What is it, my dear?" he asked. "What is troubling you?"

"I want something," answered she. "But I won't tell you what it is because I know you won't get it for me."

The dragon was hurt.

"Have I ever refused to get you what you want?" he asked. "Please tell me."

And he coaxed and begged so hard that at last his wife said,

"I have heard that monkeys' hearts are delicious. I long to eat a monkey's heart. If I don't, I know I shall die."

The poor dragon was terrified at the thought of losing his wife. But a monkey's heart! How could he ever get that?

"You know the monkeys live high in the trees, deep in the forests. How could I ever reach them?" he said.

"There," said the wife, beginning to cry. "I knew you didn't mean it when you said you'd do anything for me. You don't really care for me at all. And now I shall surely die."

The dragon didn't know what to do. Finally he said to himself, "One can only try." So he left the great China sea, went ashore, and journeyed until he came to a forest. There, way up in a tree, he spied a frisky monkey.

"Good afternoon, pretty one," he said, sweetly. "That is a very tall tree you're in. Aren't you afraid you'll fall out?"

"Me—fall out of a tree!" The monkey burst out laughing. "Ha, ha, ha!" he laughed. "Who ever heard of such a thing?"

The dragon tried again.

"That isn't a very juicy-looking tree," he said, more sweetly than before. "I know a forest full of trees laden with ripe, juicy fruit. It's only across the sea."

"You are indeed a foolish dragon," said the monkey. "What you say is all very well, but how would I cross the sea?"

"Why," said the dragon innocently, "all you have to do is get on my back and I'll swim across with you."

So the little monkey came down and climbed up on the dragon's back. He, of course, lost no time in striking out for the China sea. When they were half-way across, the dragon suddenly dived down beneath the water.

"Where are you going? What are you doing?" cried the monkey in alarm.

"I might as well tell you now," said the dragon. "There is no forest and no trees and no juicy fruit. There is only my wife who is ill and who says nothing but a monkey's heart will cure her. And so I am trying to drown you."

The monkey thought fast and quick. "My dear

friend," he said, "why didn't you tell me before we started out? Gladly would I give up my heart to help your wife. But, don't you know that monkeys never carry their hearts around with them? I left mine in the tree where you found me. However, if you don't mind going back, I'll be happy to fetch it for you at once."

The dragon turned around and went back to the forest and the very tree where he first saw the monkey. The little monkey, with a leap and a bound, was soon safe in the topmost branch. The dragon waited and waited, and begged and begged the monkey to come down with his heart. But the monkey didn't even bother to answer him. And for all I know that foolish dragon is still waiting there. Perhaps in time he will learn that monkeys carry with them not only their hearts but their clever thinking caps too.

The Wise King and the Little Bee

Retold by Rose Dobbs

Many, many years ago there lived in the holy city of Jerusalem a mighty king whose name was Solomon. And his fame was in all the nations round about. For God had given Solomon a wise and understanding heart. He was wiser than any man who lived before him and any man who came after. And all the earth sought the presence of Solomon to hear his wisdom, and he always judged wisely and well.

Now, suppose I were to tell you that a little bee, a little, tiny, insignificant bee, once proved itself to be wiser than this wisest of men? You would probably not believe it. Yet it is true. There is an old, old story to prove it, and because Solomon was humble as he was wise, the story has a happy ending. And here it is:

It happened that among the countries which rang with the fame of Solomon's wisdom and riches was the country over which ruled the proud and beautiful Queen of Sheba. She longed to prove to everyone that Solomon was not the wisest man in the world. She would have liked to set him some difficult task which he could not perform, or better still, ask him a simple question which he would not be able to answer. She thought and she thought and at last an idea came to her.

She called together all the most skilled craftsmen in the land, and she commanded them to fashion for her a bouquet of flowers. It was to be of roses of Sharon and lilies of the valley. And the flowers were to be made so beautifully, so perfectly, that no one standing within a few inches of them would be able to tell if they were real or false. The craftsmen went to work and shortly afterwards brought the bouquet to the queen. The little bells of the lilies of the valley and the purple blossoms of the roses of Sharon were so perfect that the queen could not believe they were not real. And her skilled workmen had labored long and hard to distil a perfume that matched perfectly the fragrance of the real flowers.

The queen was more than pleased. "Now we shall see," said she, "how wise Solomon truly is."

So she announced that she would pay him a visit; to do him honor, she said. And she came to Jerusalem with a very great train, with camels that bore spices and much gold, and with boxes full of precious stones.

Solomon received her graciously. The best rooms in the palace were offered to her and her companions. The finest musicians and dancers entertained her. And a lavish banquet was planned for her. On the evening of the banquet, the queen sent her most trusted servant to procure a bouquet of real roses of Sharon and lilies of the valley. When the merry-making and feasting were in full swing, the queen left the gay company and soon returned with the two bouquets. Everyone gasped. Never had they seen such beautiful bouquets, such perfect flowers, and one the exact copy of the other.

"O, great and mighty king," said the Queen of Sheba, standing at a little distance from Solomon and holding out the two bouquets, "the whole world rings with stories of your wisdom. Tell me, you who can always see the truth, which of these bouquets is made up of real flowers and which of false?"

There was a deep silence in the vast hall. Not one person there could see any difference between the two bouquets. The little white bells of the lilies of the valley swayed gently in each and the lovely purple blossoms of the roses of Sharon sent out a faint perfume from each.

The deep silence was broken by a whispering and murmuring which started in one corner, traveled to another and soon filled the vast hall. Solomon leaned forward and wrinkled his brow. He heard the excited and anxious mutterings of his people, but both bouquets looked exactly alike. Perhaps they were both real? Or, perhaps they were both false? Suddenly, above the hum in the hall, Solomon's sharp ear caught another sound. It was made by a little bee buzzing against a window. Solomon smiled. He was wise enough to know that all wisdom comes from God and that God has given to each of His creatures a special wisdom of its own. So he motioned to one of his servants to open the window. No sooner was this done than the bee flew into the room. The king's eyes followed it. Straight and sure it flew to one of the bouquets and was soon lost to sight deep within the blossoms. So engrossed in watching the queen or in whispering to each other were the people that no one noticed what had happened.

The king sat up very straight and met the queen's mocking eyes.

"My gracious and honored guest," he said, "the true flowers are those," and he pointed to the bouquet chosen by the little bee.

The queen was astonished.

"It was a true report that I heard in my own land of your acts and of your wisdom," she said. "But I did not believe the words, until I came and have myself seen it. You have wisdom beyond the fame of which I have heard. Happy are your men, happy are your servants, happy are all those who stand before you always and hear your wisdom."

Then a great shout and roar of praise rang out from all the people. But the king himself was silent. In his heart he was giving thanks for the little bee that had come to help him.

The Lion-Makers

Translated by Arthur W. Ryder
from Tales of the Panchantantra

In a certain town were four Brahmins, that is to say, four very educated men. They were great friends. Three of them were famous scholars, but they had no common sense. The fourth had never been able to learn anything at all. He had nothing *but* common sense.

One day the four friends met to talk things over.

"What is the use of knowing a lot," said they, "and

being very smart, if one does not travel, win the favor of kings, and make a lot of money? Whatever we do, let us all travel."

So they set out. But when they had gone a little way, the eldest of them said,

"One of us, the fourth, is a stupid fellow. He has nothing but sense. Now nobody gains the favorable attention of kings just by having common sense. One must be a scholar too. Therefore, I don't think we ought to share our earnings with him. Let him turn back and go home."

Then the second Brahmin turned to the man of sense and said, "You know this is true. Please go home."

But the third said, "No, no. This is no way to behave, for we have been friends and played together since we were little boys. Come along, my good friend. You shall have a share of the money we earn."

To this the others at last agreed and they continued on their journey. Soon they came to a forest and there in front of them lay the bones of a dead lion.

Then one of the educated men said, "Here is a good chance to show how much we know. Here lies some kind of creature, dead. Let us bring it to life by means of all we have learned."

25

The first Brahmin said, "I know how to put together the skeleton."

The second said, "I can give it skin, flesh, and blood."

The third said, "I can give it life."

So the first put together all the bones. The second gave it skin, flesh, and blood. But while the third was busy breathing life into it, the fourth, the man of common sense, spoke up.

"My worthy and learned friends," he said, "common sense would tell us that this creature is a lion. I would not advise you to bring it to life. If you do, he will surely eat every one of us."

The Brahmins were very angry. "You simpleton!" they said. "Are you trying to tell us that you know more than we do?"

"I only know what my common sense tells me," said the fourth Brahmin. "However, if you insist on going ahead, just wait until I climb this convenient tree."

After the fourth Brahmin climbed up the tree, the lion was brought to life. He rose up, opened wide his jaws, and ate up all three scholars.

But the man of sense, after the lion had gone off, climbed down from the tree and went home.

The Happy Cure

Retold by Rose Dobbs

A foolish king lay dying. At least, that's what he said. Yes, he said he was at death's door. But the truth of the matter was this: the king was suffering from having nothing to do. He was being bored to death.

Of course, the king would not admit this. He groaned and moaned and complained of sharp stabs in every muscle and sticking pains in every bone in his body. Physicians and surgeons came from far and wide. They looked down the king's throat, they tapped his chest, and they felt his pulse. They hemmed and hawed and stroked their beards. But they could find nothing wrong.

"Physicians and surgeons are dolts," cried the king. "Aren't there any plain ordinary doctors in the kingdom?"

The plain ordinary doctors came from hither and yon. They felt the king's pulse, tapped his chest, and looked down his throat. They hawed and hemmed, took off their spectacles, put them on again. But they could find nothing wrong.

"Plain ordinary doctors are idiots," cried the king in a rage. "The next one who examines me and finds nothing wrong will have his ears cut off and his nose shortened."

Well, you would think that would have put a stop to the coming of the doctors and the surgeons and the physicians. But no. The king kept sending messengers and couriers to bring them in. The people were in despair. Such an epidemic of heads without ears and faces with shortened noses had never been seen!

Finally a simple old woman came to see the king. The exhausted prime minister brought her into the royal bedchamber.

The simple old woman peered into the king's face for a long time. Then she said, "Your Majesty, you ar

28

uffering from a strange and rare disease. So rare and trange, that no name exists for it."

"There, I knew it," cried the king in glee. "I kept telling all of them, the fools, that I'm a sick man."

"A very sick man," said the simple old woman.

The king leaned back among his silken pillows and

29

closed his eyes and wrinkled his brow as if he were in pain.

"And is there no cure for me?" he asked.

"Oh, yes, your Majesty. You need sleep but one night in the shirt of a happy man and you will be cured instantly," said the simple old woman.

The king summoned the captain of his guard and his bravest soldiers; the best couriers in the land; and the swiftest messengers and heralds.

"Start off at once," he commanded them, "and bring me back the shirt of a happy man. And mind you don't return without it," he added darkly.

The soldiers and couriers, messengers and heralds traveled far and wide from east to west, from north to south, across seas and deserts; through cities and over mountains, from one end of the kingdom to the other. But nowhere could they find a happy man. They sent long reports to the king. And this is what the reports said:

The people in the east might be happy if your Majesty didn't tax them so heavily.

And, the people in the west might be happy if they didn't have to work so long and so hard, so they might have a little time to enjoy music and singing and dancing.

And, the people in the north might be happy if sometimes they could see your Majesty and felt you were interested in them.

And, the people in the south might be happy if your Majesty would notice their industry and faithfulness and would reward them.

The king read the reports hastily and flung them away. But as time went by and none of the messengers returned, and more and more reports came to him of a people that might be happy if their king so chose, he began to read more carefully.

One day a little stableboy, wandering about the palace grounds, came upon a man sitting under a tree in the royal garden. He was singing lustily.

The little stableboy approached him.

"Good afternoon," he said politely. "What makes you sing so merrily?"

"I sing from joy," said the stranger. "I love my fellow man, I own but little and want less. I am a happy man and therefore I sing."

"A happy man," cried the little stableboy. "Oh, do you

not know then that the whole kingdom is looking for you? Do you not know that the king is very ill and only if he can sleep one night in the shirt of a happy man can he be cured? Quick, quick, take off your shirt! Quick, quick, give it to me."

The man burst into laughter. "My shirt," he gasped. "Why, you little ragamuffin, I don't possess a shirt." And jumping to his feet, he gathered his tattered coat about him and walked off.

The little stableboy flew to the palace. Past the guards and the prime minister he sped, right into the royal bed-chamber.

"Well, what have we here?" cried the king.

The little stableboy had to wait until he recovered his breath before he could talk.

"Oh, your Majesty," he cried. "The cure was right here all the time—right at hand—right on the palace grounds. I found him—he said he loved his fellow man, owned but little and wanted less. But," and the little boy's lips trembled, "but he didn't possess a shirt."

Then the king hung his head, ashamed to meet the clear eyes of the little stableboy.

"Yes, the cure has been here all the time," he murmured. "Only I can cure my own folly."

And he resolved then and there to be a good king, to help his people, to rule wisely and well. He never fancied himself ill again for he became too busy for such foolishness, and so he lived to a ripe old age.

The Clever Peasant

Translated from the Italian by T. F. Crane

There was once a king who, while hunting, saw a peasant working in the fields and asked him: "How much do you earn in a day?"

"Four *carlini,* your Majesty," answered the peasant.

"What do you do with them?" continued the king.

The peasant said: "The first I eat; the second I put out to interest; the third I give back, and the fourth I throw away."

The king rode on, but after a time the peasant's answer seemed very curious to him, so he returned and asked him:

"Tell me, what do you mean by eating the first *carlino,* putting the second out to interest, giving back the third, and throwing away the fourth?"

34

The peasant answered: "With the first I feed myself; with the second I feed my children, who must care for me when I am old; with the third I feed my father, and so repay him for what he has done for me, and with the fourth I feed my wife, and thus throw it away, because I have no profit from it."

"Yes," said the king, "you are right. Promise me, however, that you will not tell anyone this until you have seen my face a hundred times."

The peasant promised and the king rode home well pleased.

While sitting at table with his ministers, he said: "I will give you a riddle. A peasant earns four *carlini* a day. The first he eats; the second he puts out at interest; the third he gives back, and the fourth he throws away. What is that?"

No one was able to answer it.

One of the ministers remembered finally that the king had spoken the day before with the peasant, and he resolved to find the peasant and obtain from him the answer.

When he saw the peasant he asked him for the answer to the riddle, but the peasant answered: "I cannot tell you, for I promised the king to tell no one until I have seen his face a hundred times."

"Oh!" said the minister, "I can show you the king's face," and he drew a hundred coins from his purse and gave them to the peasant. On every coin the king's face was to be seen, of course. After the peasant had looked at each coin once, he said: "I have now seen the king's face a hundred times, and can tell you the answer to the riddle." And he told him it.

The minister went in great glee to the king and said: "Your Majesty, I have found the answer to the riddle. It is so and so."

The king exclaimed: "You can have heard it only from the peasant himself." He had the peasant summoned, and took him to task.

"Did you not promise me not to tell until you had seen my face a hundred times?" he asked.

"But, your Majesty," answered the peasant, "your minister showed me your picture a hundred times."

Then he showed him the bag of money that the minister had given him. The king was so pleased with the clever peasant that he rewarded him, and made him a rich man for the rest of his life.

Please All—Please None

Retold by Rose Dobbs

It happened once upon a time that a man and his young son were on their way to market. With them was their donkey. And so they walked along—the donkey in the middle, the man on one side, the boy on the other.

The way was long, the sun hot. As the three ambled on, the man and boy stopped often to wipe the sweat from their brows.

"Now aren't you two the silly ones!" exclaimed a farmer who saw them. "What is a donkey for if not to ride upon?"

So the man put his little son on the donkey, and they went on. They had not gone very far when they met several country people.

"What is the world coming to?" cried out one of them. "Have children no pity at all for their parents? Just see this great big lazy boy. He rides in comfort while his poor old father must toil in the dust and heat."

The man told the boy to get off and he himself got on the donkey. But they hadn't gone very far when they met a husband and wife.

"For shame," cried they. "Only a selfish father would

ride on a hot day like this while his poor little son needs must trudge after."

The man stopped and scratched his head. What was he to do? Finally he took the boy up in front of him on the donkey. And they continued on their way. Soon they reached the outskirts of the town. Everyone they met pointed their fingers at them and cried, "Shame! Shame!"

"Now what is wrong?" asked the man.

"What indeed?" said the townspeople. "Anyone can see you give never a thought to the donkey. Because the poor animal cannot speak for himself, is that any reason why you and your hulking son must abuse him? How do you suppose he likes the burden of both of you on so hot a day?"

The man and the boy both jumped off the donkey. What should they do now? They thought for a long, long time, and at last an idea came to them. They cut down a pole, tied the donkey's feet to it, raised pole and donkey to their shoulders, and once more went on their way.

But at every turn they were greeted by shouts and laughter.

"See the old fool, and the young one too," cried everyone. "It's easy to tell which is the donkey in this group."

Accompanied by such remarks, the three went along until they reached a little bridge which spanned the market stream. Here the donkey, frightened by all the shouts and laughter, pulled hard at his bonds, got one of his feet loose, and kicked out. This made the boy drop his end of the pole. In the struggle that followed, the donkey fell over the bridge, into the water. As his forefeet were still tied together, he could not swim to the shore, and so he was drowned.

The man sighed sadly. "That will teach me a lesson," he said. "If you try to please everybody, you please nobody, and you lose what you have into the bargain."

Part II: *Why and How*

Why Pigs Have Curly Tails

By Rose Fyleman

There was once a fairy who fell into a bramble-bush. It was a very closely grown bush, and she could not get out. She was sadly scratched, and the thorns caught her delicate wings and tore her pretty frail dress into shreds.

The bramble-bush formed part of a hedge which ran along the side of an orchard, and presently a horse came sauntering up to the hedge.

"Oh, please help me, sir," said the fairy. "I'm caught in a bramble-bush, and can't get out."

The horse came and looked at her.

"That's a nasty place to be in," he said. "What will you give me if I get you out?"

45

"I'll give you a golden halter and a silver bit," said the fairy.

The horse shook his head. "It's not worth it," he said. "I should scratch my face. My master loves me for my beautiful satin skin, and I really can't risk spoiling my appearance. Besides, I have some very nice harness of my own. He sees to that. Sorry I can't be of any assistance." And he ambled away.

A little later a robin perched on the bramble-bush.

"Oh, please, Mr. Robin, won't you come and help me?" said the fairy. "I can't get out."

"What will you give me," said the robin, "if I help you out?"

"I'll give you a jacket of gold and slippers of silver," said the fairy.

"Thank you very much," said the robin, "but I don't think that's quite my style. I have a nice red waistcoat already and I should hate to look gaudy. Besides, I am tremendously busy. I've got a young family to look after, and my wife doesn't like me to be away long." And he flew off.

There were sheep grazing in the field on the other side

46

of the hedge, and one of them came munching close to the bramble-bush.

"Oh, please, Mrs. Sheep," said the fairy, "can you help me out of here?"

"What will you give if I do?" said the sheep.

"I will teach you to sing as the fairies sing," said the fairy. "I will also give you wisdom." For she was getting more and more anxious, and she thought such lovely gifts would tempt the sheep.

But the sheep stared stupidly with her glassy eyes.

"That's all very well," she replied, "but I happen to have a very nice voice naturally and can already sing rather well. As for wisdom, I don't quite know what that is, but I don't think it sounds very interesting. I'd help you gladly, but the thorns would tear my fine woolen coat, and that would never do. Surely a fine woolen coat is worth more than wisdom." And she moved away.

The fairy was beginning to despair; she thought she would never, never be able to get back to Fairyland. But just as she had given up hope, a pig came wandering past, making ugly noises and staring about with his little blue eyes. He spied the fairy sitting in the midst of the bramble-bush with her head down on her knees.

"What's the matter?" said the pig.

The fairy raised her head and saw the pig's ugly pink snout poking in between the bramble-twigs.

"I think I can get you out," he said, when she had told him her trouble. "I'm not much to look at, but I've got a good tough hide, and at any rate I shan't be afraid of a few scratches spoiling my beauty." So with a good many snuffles and grunts he pushed his head and shoulders well into the middle of the bush and made a clear way for the fairy to get out.

She gave a sigh of relief when she found herself once more free and in the clear sunshine, and the pig stood and looked at her admiringly, for she was a dear little thing. He was so conscious of his ugliness beside her pretty grace that he turned away and started off down the orchard.

"Don't go—oh, don't go," said the fairy.

The pig turned around.

"You've not had your reward," said the fairy.

"I don't want any reward, thank you," grunted the pig, and moved on.

48

But the fairy persisted. She flew after him. "You must have a reward," she said. "I shall be most unhappy, if you don't."

"But I don't want anything, thank you," said the pig. "I have been more than glad to help you."

The fairy stood in front of him, anxiously pondering as to what she could possibly give him that might be of any use. Nobody seemed to want her fairy gifts. She looked him up and down.

"Wouldn't you like something—something to make you more beautiful?" she said.

She really meant less ugly, but she was so grateful to the pig that she was very anxious not to hurt his feelings, and so she put it that way.

"I'm afraid it's rather hopeless," said the pig, with half a smile. "You see, I'm such an ugly fellow. You'd have to alter me all over."

"But surely—a little something . . ." said the fairy, and she looked at him more thoughtfully than ever.

Now all this happened a very long time ago when pigs had quite straight tails like most of the other animals, and suddenly, looking at his tail, the fairy had an idea.

"I know, I know," she said. "You shall have a curly tail. It will be an immense improvement, and *so* uncommon."

The pig looked rather pleased. "Well, have it your own way," he said. "I can't see my own tail, in any case, but I dare say it wouldn't look bad."

So the fairy touched the pig's tail with her wand, and it instantly curled up into nice little rings.

Ever since that day pigs have had curly tails, and now you know how they came by this beautiful adornment.

How the Milky Way Began

By Eva Knox Evans

Look almost directly above you. You will see a white band of light that trails clear across the sky. That is the Milky Way. It looks like a million tiny grains of dust. But the Milky Way is really a great band of individual stars. Some are very large. Some are a little smaller. And here is a story, told sometimes in Persia, sometimes in Africa, of the way the Milky Way began:

Once there lived a man who was both greedy and sly.

If he needed a thing, like a horse or a sheep, he would not work to get it. He would steal it from his neighbors instead.

Now, one day, this man needed a load of straw. He could have harvested the fields as his neighbors did, but instead he took his horse and cart, crept into his neighbor's field in the dead of night, and stole that load of straw.

Since he was unused to work, he took some time to load the straw in his wagon. By the time he had finished, the great golden sun was beginning its climb across the sky, and all the people were waking from their dark night of sleep. Where was he to hide his great load of straw so that it could not be seen?

He looked this way and he looked that way, but could find no place to hide his wagon. Then he looked up, and there was the wide, blue sky above him, and no one was in it at all. The very place to hide! He lashed his horse, and away he flew. Up, up, he went, until he was sailing across the very middle of the sky! He flew fast and faster so that no one might see where he was hiding his precious load.

The day passed, and when the sun had made his trip

across the blue sky and settled behind the hills of the earth, lo! and behold! the man had disappeared and his stolen straw with him. Now, no one would find him.

But wait a moment! The man, as you know, had hurried across the sky, and as he hurried, some pieces of the straw had dropped out of his cart. There they were across the middle of the sky, showing the path he had gone.

Look up into the sky any clear night, and you will see —a golden path of shining straw. You may not be able to find the man, the man who was greedy and sly. But you know which way he went.

Why No One Ever Carries the Alligator Down to the Water

By Blaise Cendrars
Translated from the French by Margery Bianco

Bama, the alligator, said: "I am hungry."

And he came out of the water with his children to look for something to eat. The water immediately began to withdraw, until it was a long, long way behind them.

There on the dry ground they yawned with hunger, their mouths open, wide open, Bama and his little alligators.

Crick! Crack! They snapped their jaws.

A hunter came by.

He said: "Bama, how-come you got out of the water?"

The alligator said: "I came to take a walk, to take a walk with my children, and all at once the water went down and it went a long, long way off behind us. Crick! Crack! I'm hungry."

The hunter said: "If you weren't such an ungrateful creature I would go and put you back in the water, you and your children."

"Oh, yes!" cried Bama. "Carry us back to the water quick, me and my children!"

So the hunter made a rope from the bark of a tree, and tied the alligator up so that he could carry him on his head, and he tied the little alligators as well by their tails, so he could carry them more easily to the river's edge.

When he reached the edge of the water, the hunter asked:

"Shall I put you down here, Bama?"

The alligator replied: "Go a little further."

The man took three steps in the water, and then said:

"Shall I put you down here, Bama?"

The alligator said: "Just a little further!"

The man took three more steps. Now the water was halfway up his legs. He said:

"Alligator, alligator, shall I put you down here?"

Bama said: "Yes, put me down here."

The hunter set him down in the water and untied him, him and his children.

Immediately the alligator caught hold of him by one foot. "Now I've got you!" he cried. "What a fine mouthful! I'm hungry. I'm going to eat you!"

"Let me go!" cried the man.

"No, I won't let you go!" said Bama. "I'm hungry."

"Here, let me go!" cried the man, struggling.

But Bama and the alligator children held on tight.

Then the hunter said: "Bama, I maintain that you are an ungrateful creature!"

And he kept quiet. The water was already up to his middle. The hunter stood quite still, and he did not speak again.

A little hare came by. He said: "Hunter, why are you standing so still, there?"

The man answered: "Bama has hold of me."

"Why did the alligator catch hold of you?" asked the little hare.

The man spoke very quickly, for he was beginning to get frightened, and he told the little hare everything that had happened.

"And now when I cry out 'Let me go, let me go!'" he said, "they answer 'No, we shan't let you go!' Do you think that's fair?"

The little hare said: "Were you able to carry that great big alligator on your head?"

The hunter said: "Yes, the big one!"

"With all his children?"

"With all his children."

"You were able to carry them right down to the water?"

"Yes, I was able to."

"I don't believe it," said the little hare. And he shouted: "You, Bama, is it true what he says?"

The alligator replied: "It is the truth."

The little hare said to the man: "You know, I can't believe it unless I see you do it!" And he called to the alligator:

"Bama, will you let him carry you on his head again?"

The alligator said: "I'm quite willing!"

Then the hunter bound the alligator with his rope so as to carry him on his head again, and he gathered up all the little alligator children and tied them by their tails, and so carried them easily to the place where he had found them the first time, a long way off, beyond the water, far from the river's edge.

When he got there he was just about to untie them, so as to put them down again in the same spot, when the little hare said:

"Kill them, stupid, and eat them!"

So the man killed Bama and all the little alligators. He carried the flesh to his house and there he told the story of what had happened to him.

Ever since then, no one will carry an alligator down to the water any more. They are too ungrateful.

Why the Bananas Belong to the Monkey

By Elsie Spicer Eells

Perhaps you do not know it, but the monkeys think that all the bananas belong to them. When Brazilian children eat bananas they say, "I am a monkey." I once knew a little boy in Brazil who was very, very fond of bananas. He always said, "I am *very much* of a monkey." If you are fond of bananas the Brazilian children would tell you that you are a monkey, too. This is the story they tell to show us how it all came about.

Once upon a time when the world had just been made and there was only one kind of banana, but very many kinds of monkeys, there was a little old woman who had a big garden full of banana trees. It was very difficult for the old woman to gather the bananas herself, so she made a bargain with the largest monkey. She told him that if he would gather the bunches of bananas for her she would give him half of them. The monkey gathered the bananas. When he took his half he gave the little old woman the bananas which grow at the bottom of the bunch and are small and wrinkled. The nice big fat ones he kept for himself and carried them home to let them ripen in the dark.

The little old woman was very angry. She lay awake all night trying to think of some way by which she could get even with the monkey. At last she thought of a trick.

The next morning she made an image of wax which looked just like a little black boy. Then she placed a large flat basket on the top of the image's head and in the basket she placed the best ripe bananas she could find. They certainly looked very tempting.

After a while the biggest monkey passed that way. He saw the image of wax and thought that it was a boy peddling bananas. He had often pushed over boy banana peddlers, upset their baskets and then had run away with

the bananas. This morning he was feeling very good-natured so he thought that he would first try asking politely for the bananas.

"O, peddler boy, peddler boy," he said to him, "please give me a banana."

The image of wax answered never a word.

Again the monkey said, this time in a little louder voice, "O, peddler boy, peddler boy, please give me a banana, just one little, ripe little, sweet little banana."

The image of wax answered never a word.

Then the monkey called out in his loudest voice, "O, peddler boy, peddler boy, if you don't give me a banana I'll give you such a push that it will upset all of your bananas."

The image of wax was silent.

The monkey ran toward the image of wax and struck it hard with his hand. His hand remained firmly embedded in the wax.

"O, peddler boy, peddler boy, let go my hand," the monkey called out. "Let go my hand and give me a banana or else I'll give you a hard, hard blow with my other hand." The image of wax did not let go.

The monkey gave the image a hard, hard blow with

his other hand. The other hand remained firmly embedded in the wax.

Then the monkey called out, "O, peddler boy, peddler boy, let go my two hands. Let go my two hands
and give me a banana or else I will give you a kick with
my foot."

The image of wax did not let go.

The monkey gave the image a kick with his foot and
his foot remained stuck fast in the wax.

"O, peddler boy, peddler boy," the monkey cried, "let
go my foot. Let go my two hands and my foot and give
me a banana or else I'll give you a kick with my other
foot." The image of wax did not let go.

Then the monkey who was now very angry, gave the
image of wax a kick with his other foot and his other
foot remained stuck fast in the wax.

The monkey shouted, "O, peddler boy, peddler boy,
let go my foot. Let go my two feet and my two hands
and give me a banana or else I'll give you a push with
my body."

The image of wax did not let go.

The monkey gave the image of wax a push with his
body. His body remained caught fast in the wax.

64

"O, peddler boy, peddler boy," the monkey shouted, "let go my body! Let go my body and my two feet and my two hands or I'll call all the other monkeys to help me!"

The image of wax did not let go.

Then the monkey made such an uproar with his cries and shouts that very soon monkeys came running from all directions. There were big monkeys and little monkeys and middle-sized monkeys. A whole army of monkeys had come to the aid of the biggest monkey.

It was the very littlest monkey who thought of a plan to help the biggest monkey out of his plight. The monkeys were to climb up into the biggest tree and pile themselves one on top of another until they made a pyramid of monkeys. The monkey with the very loudest voice of all was to be on top and he was to shout his very loudest to the sun and ask the sun to come and help the biggest monkey out of his dreadful difficulty.

This is what all the big-sized, little-sized, and middle-sized monkeys did. The monkey with the loudest voice on top of the pyramid made the sun hear. The sun came at once.

The sun poured his hottest rays down upon the wax.

After a while the wax began to melt. The monkey was at last able to pull out one of his hands. The sun poured down more of his hottest rays and soon the monkey was able to pull out his two hands. Then he could pull out one foot, then another, and in a little while his body, too. At last he was free.

When the little old woman saw what had happened she was very much discouraged about raising bananas. She decided to move to another part of the world where she raised cabbages instead of bananas. The monkeys were left in possession of the big garden full of banana trees. From that day to this the monkeys have thought that they owned all the bananas.

Why Cats Always Wash Themselves After Eating

Retold by Rose Dobbs

Once upon a time a hungry cat went out to look for something special to eat. She did not want a little mouse and she did not want a saucer of milk and she did not want a juicy fishhead. She wanted something special, something different. All of a sudden she saw in front of her a little bird.

"Aha!" thought the cat. "That's exactly what I want. What a delicious meal that bird will make."

So she approached softly, crouched very low, and slunk along the ground until she came close to the bird. The bird, too, was looking for something to eat, and it was so busy digging for worms that it didn't hear the cat. (Alas, that's the way things go in this world! Cats eat birds and birds eat worms and worms—but let us get on with the story.)

Suddenly the cat leaped forward and in the twinkling of an eye the bird was held fast between her paws. The poor little bird was so frightened that it was scarcely able to breathe. The cat's whiskers twitched happily as she thought of the fine meal she would soon have. But first she wanted a little fun. So she teased the bird, pushing it this way and that, pretending to let it go and snatching it back again. In the meantime, the little bird began to recover its breath and its wits.

Just as the cat opened her mouth to eat it, the bird spoke up:

"Are you going to eat me now?" it asked politely.

"Certainly," said the cat, "and it won't do you any good to object."

"Oh, I'm not objecting," said the bird. "I'm merely disappointed. It's bad enough to be eaten by a cat but it's positively humiliating to be eaten by a cat of no manners."

"No manners," cried the cat in a huff, "who says I have no manners?"

68

"I have spent much time flying about," said the bird, "and I've been everywhere from the humblest cottage to the king's palace itself. Nowhere have I ever seen a cat—not even a brand-new kitten—ever begin a meal without washing first. It's simply out of the question in polite society."

The cat sat up proudly. "I know as well as any cat in the land," she said haughtily, "that one must wash before one eats. Now you just wait a moment." She let go of the bird and began to wash herself. Of course the bird, the moment it felt itself free, flew to safety to a near-by tree. The cat looked after it hungrily. "I deserve no better," she said to herself, "for believing so easily everything I hear."

And since that time, cats always eat first and wash afterwards.

How the Letter X Got into the Alphabet

By Carl Sandburg

(There are six hundred different stories told in the Rootabaga Country about the first time the letter X got into the alphabet and how and why it was. Here is one.)

Pig Wisps

There was an oyster king far in the south who knew how to open oysters and pick out the pearls.

He grew rich and all kinds of money came rolling in on him because he was a great oyster opener and knew how to pick out the pearls.

70

The son of this oyster king was named Shovel Ears. And it was hard for him to remember.

"He knows how to open oysters but he forgets to pick out the pearls," said the father of Shovel Ears. "He is learning to remember worse and worse and to forget better and better," said the father of Shovel Ears.

Now in that same place far in the south was a little girl with two braids of hair twisted down her back and a face saying, "Here we come—where from?"

And her mother called her Pig Wisps.

Twice a week Pig Wisps ran to the butcher shop for a soup bone. Before starting she crossed her fingers and then the whole way to the butcher shop she kept her fingers crossed.

If she met any playmates and they asked her to stop and play crosstag or jackstraws or all-around-the-mulberry-bush or the-green-grass-grew-all-around or drop the handkerchief, she told them, "My fingers are crossed and I am running to the butcher shop for a soup bone."

One morning running to the butcher shop she bumped into a big queer boy and she bumped him clear on the sidewalk.

"Did you look where you were running?" she asked him.

"I forgot again," said Shovel Ears. "I remember worse and worse. I forget better and better."

"Cross your fingers like this," said Pig Wisps, showing him how.

He ran to the butcher shop with her, watching her keep her fingers crossed till the butcher gave her the soup bone.

"After I get it then the soup bone reminds me to go home with it," she told him. "But until I get the soup bone I keep my fingers crossed."

Shovel Ears went to his father and began helping his father open oysters. And Shovel Ears kept his fingers crossed to remind him to pick out the pearls.

He picked a hundred buckets of pearls the first day and brought his father the longest, slippery, shining rope of pearls ever seen in that oyster country.

"How do you do it?" his father asked.

"It is the crossed fingers—like this," said Shovel Ears, crossing his fingers like the letter X. "This is the way to remember better and forget worse."

It was then the oyster king went and told the men who change the alphabets just what happened.

When the men who change the alphabets heard just what happened, they decided to put in a new letter, the letter X, near the end of the alphabet, the sign of the crossed fingers.

Part III: *Just for Fun*

The Number of Spots

By Geraldine Elliott

Leopard gazed at his reflection in the Looking-Pool above the waterfall and told himself for the hundredth time that his coat was truly magnificent. Those spots . . . yes, they really were superb!

Suddenly the stillness of the pool was broken as an ugly, flat head appeared above the surface. In alarm, Leopard jumped back. He had not expected to find Crocodile there—not that Crocodile was likely to take liberties with *him,* but, well, you never could tell with crocodiles.

"Ha!" barked Crocodile nastily. "Gazing at yourself as usual, I see. Vain creature!"

"You'd be vain if you'd been given the lovely spots that I have," replied Leopard with dignity.

"Spots—pah! Who wants spots? What's the good of spots, I'd like to know," said Crocodile.

"You'd soon find out if you lived in the woods instead of in the river," replied Leopard.

"The river's a very good place, thank you—or it would be if you didn't come here so often to gaze at your silly self." Crocodile snorted. "I wonder you don't count your precious spots! Or perhaps you have? How many of the pretty things are there?" he inquired with a sneer.

"I don't know. I never thought of counting," said Leopard as he turned the idea over in his mind and found it good. "Now that you have suggested it, I should very much like to know. But I don't see how I can count them for myself." Leopard wasn't going to admit that he did not know how to count, and he wondered if, by any chance, Crocodile knew.

"Would you like to count them for me?" he asked.

"No, I would not!" barked Crocodile. "I've something better to do than to waste my time counting spots." And with a vicious swirl of his tail, Crocodile turned and slipped beneath the surface of the water.

"I bet that means Crocodile can't count," chuckled Leopard as he stalked up the river bank and wandered into the woods, where he happened to meet Wart-hog. "Morning, Wart-hog!" he called out. "I suppose you wouldn't care to count my spots for me, would you?"

"What, me? Count? One-two-three-four?"

"Yes, that's it," cried Leopard excitedly. "What luck that you know how!"

"But I don't," said the surprised Wart-hog. "Whatever made you think that?"

"You, you do! You must! . . . what you said—'one-two-something-something.' That's counting."

Wart-hog shook his head.

"It's much more difficult than that," he said earnestly. "There are things that come after 'four,' and I don't know what they are, or what they mean."

"A pity," sighed Leopard, looking very disappointed. "I wonder who would know how?"

"Ask at the Drinking-pool tonight," suggested Wart-hog. "There's sure to be someone there who could help you."

"That's an idea." Leopard brightened up at once. "I

know! I'll give a prize to anyone who can tell me how many spots I've got."

There was quite a large gathering at the Drinking-pool that night, and when the animals heard that Leopard was offering a bag of maize as a prize, they were only too eager to start counting. Elephant insisted that he should have first try, as he was the oldest and biggest animal present.

"One -two -three -four -five -six -seven -eight -nine -ten," he started, all in one breath and at a tremendous pace. Then he took another breath. "One-two-three-four-five-si . . ."

"No, no!" shrieked the other animals. "You've already got as far as ten."

Elephant frowned.

"I should be obliged if you would refrain from interrupting," he said coldly. "You have made me forget where I was . . . somewhere in the second ten, I think?"

"What do you mean, 'the second ten'?" demanded Eland.

"The numbers that come after the first ten, of course. I don't approve of those 'teen'-things and I prefer to count

ten twice, which makes twenty. It's all a Question-of-Multiplication." Elephant's air of superiority was quite insufferable, and although none of the animals knew what Elephant meant by this last remark, they were determined not to be impressed.

"Supposing you start again at the beginning," suggested Buffalo.

So Elephant began again, and when he'd counted ten twice and made it twenty he stood quite still and thought so hard that his whole face puckered up into little wrinkles. Then, slowly, he made his announcement:

"Leopard has *more* than twenty spots."

"How many more?" asked Leopard.

Again Elephant frowned.

"A good many more, I should say"—his manner was exceedingly casual. "In fact, there are so many that I haven't time to count them for you, and really I must be going." With a condescending nod he began to walk away, looking exactly as if he had an important appointment to keep, though of course he hadn't, and there was no need whatever for him to go.

"Tee-hee!" giggled a young Bushbuck. "I don't believe

Elephant can count above twenty for all the airs he gives himself!" (And Bushbuck was quite right.)

"Can *you* count above twenty?" asked Leopard, but not very hopefully.

"Me? Oh, no! I can only count four. I can do that because I know I've got four legs."

Leopard sighed. He was beginning to feel depressed.

"Can't *anyone* count better than Elephant?" he asked sadly.

"I once counted up to fifty," said Ant-bear, diffidently. "Do you think that would be enough?"

"It might. Come and try."

"Very well. Where shall I start? At the tail, I think . . . one, two, three, four, five . . . now I wonder if that ought to count as one or two spots? It's sort of double."

All the animals crowded round and looked at the spot in question. After a good deal of arguing, it was agreed that it should only count as one.

"What does that make, then?" asked Ant-bear.

"Six," said Jackal.

"Five, Ant-bear said"—this from Eland.

"Better start again," said Buffalo, in a mournful voice.

Ant-bear took his advice and got as far as eleven without any trouble.

"... twelve ... that's a very fine spot, that is! ... twelve ..."

"You've said 'twelve' once," muttered Eland.

"'Sh! Don't interrupt!"

"Oh, dear, you've put me off," complained Ant-bear. "Did I count that spot or did I not?"

"Better start again," said Buffalo, gloomily.

Ant-bear sighed and did so. This time, with some difficulty, she got as far as twenty-nine. Then she paused and thought hard for a long time.

"It's no good," she said at last. "I've forgotten what comes after twenty-nine."

"Doesn't 'thirty'?" said Tortoise. "Or is it 'forty'?"

"Thirty! That's right!" exclaimed Ant-bear joyfully. "Thirty ... now, where was I?"

"Halfway up the tail."

"Yes, but was that the twenty-ninth ... or that?" She indicated two spots and a great deal of arguing followed.

"You'll have to start again." Buffalo was almost beginning to enjoy himself.

"Start what again?" It was Rabbit who spoke. He had

only that moment arrived and knew nothing of what was going on.

Instantly all the animals began to talk at once and explain about Leopard's spots.

"Wants to know how many he's got, does he?" said Rabbit when he had, at last, managed to grasp what they were trying to say. "Well, that oughtn't to be difficult. I can tell him."

"You can?"

"Yes. It's easy. Look!" Rabbit pointed to the first spot. "This one is dark, isn't it? Now, *this* one is light. Here ...dark...here...light...dark...light...dark..." He went on until every spot had been touched.

"You see?" he said when he had finished. "Leopard has only got two spots—dark ones and light ones."

The Three Wishes

A Swedish Tale

There was once a very poor man who lived with his wife in a humble little cottage. Every day he went into the forest to chop wood. One day when he was in the forest he said to himself: "Oh, dear, I am so unhappy! I am poor, and I have to work so hard all day long. My wife is hungry and I am hungry, too. Oh, I am very unhappy indeed!"

At that moment a beautiful fairy appeared before him. She said to him, "My poor man, I heard everything that you just said. I am very sorry for you and would like to help you. Ask whatever you like, and your first three wishes shall be granted."

Then just as suddenly as she had come the fairy disappeared.

The poor man felt very happy now, and he said, "I shall go home and I shall tell my wife how the fairy has granted me three wishes."

He ran back to his cottage and called to his wife:

"Wife, Wife, I am very fortunate. I saw a fairy in the forest, and she said I could have three wishes. 'Ask for anything you like,' the fairy said, 'and your wish shall be granted!' Oh, Wife, I am so happy."

"I am happy, too," said the woman. "Come, let us go into the house, my dear, and let us decide what our wishes shall be."

The man went into the little cottage and sat down at the table.

"I am hungry, Wife," he said. "I would like some dinner. While we eat we can talk about the fairy and the three wishes."

The poor man and his wife sat down at the table and started to eat their dinner, and to talk about the good fairy's promise.

"We can ask for great riches if we want to," said the man.

"Yes," the wife agreed, "we can ask for a beautiful house."

"We can even ask for a whole empire if we want to," said the man.

And his wife replied: "Oh yes, we can ask for pearls and diamonds by the hundred."

"We can ask for a big family," the man added; "five boys and five girls."

"Oh, I would prefer six boys and four girls," insisted the wife.

The man and the woman went on talking like that, but they couldn't decide what three wishes would be the most sensible of all.

The man ate his soup in silence and looked at the dry bread on his plate. "Oh, I wish I had a great big sausage for dinner!" he said.

At that very instant a great big sausage fell onto the table. Naturally, the man was very surprised to see the sausage and so was his wife.

"Oh, Husband," the wife said, "you have been very foolish. You asked for a silly old sausage and so one of the wishes has been granted. Now there are only two wishes left."

"Yes," said the man, "I have been very foolish. But we still have two wishes. We can ask for great riches and an empire."

"Yes," his wife agreed, "we can still ask for riches and an empire, but we can't ask for ten children. And it's your fault for being so foolish. It's your fault for demanding a sausage. You would rather have a sausage than a big family."

The poor woman went on talking like that, complaining, and saying over and over again, "It's your fault for being so foolish!"

Finally the man lost his patience and said: "I am tired of your complaining! I wish that the sausage were hanging from the end of your nose!"

The next second the sausage was hanging from the end of his wife's nose. Naturally, the poor woman was greatly surprised, and so was her husband.

The woman started to complain again, more loudly than before.

"Oh, my husband," she said, "you have been very, very foolish! First you asked for a sausage and then you wished that the sausage were hanging from the end of my nose. That makes two wishes. Two foolish wishes! And we have only one left!"

"Yes," the man agreed; "but we can still ask for great riches."

"What good are riches," the woman complained, "if I have a sausage hanging from the end of my nose? Why, I look ridiculous! And it's all your fault!"

The poor woman started to cry, and the poor man said: "Oh, I wish that the sausage weren't here at all!"

Instantly the sausage disappeared, and the man and the woman were right back where they started, as poor as ever. They both complained, but it didn't do them any good, for they had used up their wishes.

The three wishes had been granted and still they had no riches, no empire, no pearls and diamonds, no little boys and no little girls.

And they didn't even have any sausage for dinner!

How Many Donkeys?

A Turkish Folktale
Retold by Alice Geer Kelsey

There was the tinkle of tiny bells, the sharp clip of small hoofs, the throaty drone of a solitary singer. Nasr-ed-din Hodja was bringing the donkeys back from the mill, their saddle bags filled with freshly ground wheat. The hot Turkish sun beat down on his turbaned head. The brown dust from the donkeys' feet puffed about him. The staccato trot of his donkey jiggled him back and forth. But Nasr-ed-din Hodja was too pleased to be uncomfortable.

"I'll show them," he chuckled. "They gave me plenty of advice about taking care of their donkeys and their

91

wheat. As though I did not know more about donkeys than any man in the village of Ak Shehir!"

His eyes rested lazily on the narrow road ahead. At first it followed the brook running from Mill Valley, the brook that turned the heavy stones to grind the wheat. Then the road disappeared over a hilltop.

"Just over that hill," he mused contentedly, "is Shehir where they are waiting for their donkeys. There is not a scratch nor a bruise on one of the little creatures. No donkeys in all Turkey have had better treatment today than these nine." Idly he began counting them.

"What?" he gasped. "Eight donkeys?"

He jumped from his donkey and ran hither and yon, looking behind rocks and over hilltops but no stray donkey could he see. At last he stood beside the donkeys and counted again. This time there were nine. With a sigh of relief he climbed onto his own donkey and went singing along the road. His long legs in their baggy trousers swung easily back and forth in time to the donkey's trot.

Passing through a cluster of trees, he thought it time to count the donkeys again.

"One—two—three—" and up to eight he counted but no ninth donkey was to be seen. Down from his donkey's back he came. Behind all the trees he peered. Not a hair of a donkey could he find.

Again he counted, standing beside his donkeys. There they all were—nine mild little donkeys waiting for orders to move on. Nasr-ed-din scratched his poor head in bewilderment. Was he losing his mind or were the donkeys bewitched? Again he counted. Yes, surely there were nine.

"Brrrr." Nasr-ed-din Hodja gave the low guttural sound which is Turkish for "Giddap."

As he rode on, he looked about him for the evil spirits which must be playing tricks on him. Each donkey wore the blue beads which should drive away the evil spirits. Were there evil spirits abroad stronger even than the blue beads?

He was glad to see a friend coming down the road.

"Oh, Mustapha," he cried, "have you seen one of these donkeys? I have lost a donkey and yet I have not lost it."

"What can you mean, Hodja?" asked Mustapha.

"I left the mill with nine donkeys," explained Hodja.

"Part of the way home there have been nine and part of the way there have been eight. Oh, I am bewitched! Help me!"

Mustapha was used to the queer ways of Hodja but was surprised at such a wailing. He counted the donkeys silently.

"Let me see you count the donkeys," he asked Hodja.

"One—two—three—" began Hodja, pointing at each one as he counted up to eight.

As he said the last number, he stopped and looked at his friend with a face full of helplessness and terror. His

terror turned to amazement as Mustapha slapped his knee and laughed until he almost fell from his own donkey.

"What is so funny?" asked Hodja.

"Oh, Nasr-ed-din Hodja," laughed Mustapha. "When you are counting your brothers, why, oh why, do you not count the brother on whom you are riding?"

Nasr-ed-din was silent for a moment to think through this discovery. Then he kissed the hand of his deliverer, and thanked him a thousand times for his help. He rode whistling on to Ak Shehir to deliver the donkeys to their owners.

Clever Elsie

By Jacob and Wilhelm Grimm
Translated by Wanda Gág

There was a man, he had a daughter who always tried to use her brains as much as possible and so she was called Clever Elsie.

When she grew up, her father said, "It is time to get her married."

And his wife said, "Yes, if only some one would come along who might want her."

At last from far away came one by name of Hans, who said, "Yes, I'll marry the girl, but only if she's really as clever as you say."

"Oh," said the father, "our Elsie is no fool."

And the mother said, "*Ei,* that's true. She is so clever, she can see the wind coming up the street. Yes, and she can hear the flies cough too."

"Well, we'll see," said Hans, "but if she's not bright I don't want her."

After they had all sat down at the table and had eaten something, the mother said, "Elsie, go down into the cellar and get us some beer."

At this the clever girl took the jug from the wall and trotted down the cellar stairs, clattering the lid smartly on the way, so as to be doing something with her time. Down in the cellar she brought out a little stool, put it in front of the cask, and sat on it, so she wouldn't have to bend over and perhaps unexpectedly hurt her back. Then she set the jug in front of the cask and turned on the tap. But while she was waiting for the jug to be filled, she did not want her eyes to remain idle, so she began busily looking around at the walls and ceiling. After much gazing hither and thither, what should she see right above her but a pickax which had been forgotten and left there by the masons! At this, Clever Elsie burst into tears, thinking: "If I should marry Hans and we should get a little baby, and he grows up and we send him down here to draw some beer, that pickax might suddenly fall down on his head and kill him."

So there she sat and cried with all her might over this possible accident.

Those up in the kitchen waited and waited for her, but she did not, did not come. At last the mother said to the hired girl, "Do go down into the cellar and see what's keeping our Clever Elsie."

When the girl went down and found Elsie sitting there, weeping so bitterly, she said, "Why are you crying like that?"

"Ach!" said Elsie. "Why shouldn't I cry? If I marry Hans and we get a baby and he's grown up and comes down here to draw some beer, maybe that pickax will fall on his head and kill him."

At this the hired girl said, "How can you think of all those things? Oh, what a clever Elsie you are, to be sure." So she sat down beside Elsie and began to cry, too, over the great misfortune.

. . . . .

After a time, as the hired girl did not return and those up in the kitchen were becoming restless and thirsty, the father said to the hired man, "You! Do you go down into the cellar and see what is keeping Elsie and the hired girl."

The hired man went down. There sat the two girls, both crying as though their hearts would break.

"What are you crying about, then?" asked the hired man.

"Ach!" said Elsie. "Why shouldn't we cry? When I marry Hans and we get a child and he's grown up and has to come down here and draw beer, this pickax might easily fall down on his head and kill him."

"Oh, what a calamity!" cried the hired man. "And what a clever Elsie you are, to be sure." So he sat down too, and kept them company with loud and anguished howls.

.   .   .   .   .

Above in the kitchen, the others were waiting for the hired man. As he didn't come and didn't come, the father said to the mother, "Wife, do you go down into the cellar and see where our Clever Elsie is staying."

The mother went down and found all three in the midst of loud lamentations. When she asked them the

reason for such grief, Elsie explained that her future child would surely be killed, in case he should come down to draw beer just as the pickax might fall down on his head.

"Oh!" said the mother. "Who but our Clever Elsie could think so far ahead?" And she sat down and joined the rest in their sobs and wails.

. . . . .

The father up in the kitchen waited a while for his wife, but as she did not return either, he said, "Well, I guess I'll have to go down there myself and see what is keeping our Clever Elsie so long."

As he went down the cellar stairs and saw all four sitting there and crying, he asked them what was the matter. And when he heard that the reason for their grief was a child which Elsie might have some day, and which might be killed in case the pickax should fall down just at the time the child might be sitting there drawing beer, he cried, "Ah! That is foresight indeed! What a Clever Elsie we have, to be sure." And he sat down and cried too.

. . . . .

Hans, in the meantime, stayed up in the kitchen for a long time but as no one returned, he said to himself: "They'll be waiting for you down there, no doubt. You'd better go down and see what they're about."

As he went down into the cellar there sat five, moaning and howling pitifully, one always louder than the next.

"What terrible misfortune has happened down here?" cried Hans.

"Ach, dear Hans!" wept Elsie. "If you and I get married and have a baby and he grows up and we might perhaps send him down here to draw some beer, that pickax might fall on his head and kill him. Isn't that something to cry about?"

"Well!" cried Hans. "That shows deep thought. More wisdom than this is not needful for my household and, since you are really such a clever Elsie, I will marry you!"

He grabbed her by the hand, took her upstairs, and soon they were celebrating their wedding.

. . . . .

After Hans and Elsie were married and had a house and farm of their own, Hans said: "Wife, I must go out and earn some money. Do you go off into the field and reap the rye so that we may have bread."

"Yes, yes, dear Hans, that I will do," said Clever Elsie.

After he had gone she cooked up a good big broth and took it with her to the field. Once there, she sat down and began to use her brain as usual, for she wanted to be sure not to do the wrong thing. So she asked herself, "What shall I do? Shall I eat before I reap? Or shall I sleep before I reap? *Hei!* I'll eat first."

She sat down and ate up all the broth, and this made her almost too drowsy to move.

"I must put my clever brain to work," she thought to herself. "Now then, shall I sleep first or shall I reap first? Shall I reap or shall I sleep?" And so as not to waste any time while she was thinking, she began to cut down the grain.

She was now so sleepy she hardly knew what she was doing. While she was still saying, "Shall I reap? Shall I sleep? Reap or sleep? Sleep? Reap?" she began to cut off her clothes, thinking it was the rye. Apron, shirt, skirt and kirtle: all were slashed in half. But Elsie did not know it— she was still asking herself the big question, "Shall I reap first or sleep first?"

At last she found the answer. *"Hei,* I'll sleep first!" she said, tumbled down among the rye-stalks, and was soon sleeping soundly.

When she awoke it was almost dark. She got up, and seeing herself all tattered and torn, and half naked besides, she did not know herself.

"I wonder," she said, "am I, I? Or am I not I?"

Try as she would, she couldn't find the answer, so she went on, "Now you! You're very clever and you ought to know. Think hard! Are you Elsie or somebody else?'

Still she didn't know.

At last the clever girl had an idea. "I know!" she said. "I'll go home and see if I'm there or not."

So she ran home and knocked at the window and said, "Is Clever Elsie there?"

"Yes, yes," said Hans, who thought she had come home long ago, "no doubt she's in her bed fast asleep."

"Ach!" cried Clever Elsie. "Then I'm already at home, and this is not I, and I'm not Elsie but somebody else, and I don't live here."

So she ran away, and no one ever saw her after that. But as she was such a clever girl and always knew what to do, I'm sure she got along very well wherever she went.

The Stubborn Sillies

Retold by Rose Dobbs

Now you shall hear what happened to a couple who were not only stubborn, but silly as well.

A man and wife they were, and they lived a long time ago in a cottage high on a windy hill. One evening the man had just settled himself in his rocking chair with his pipe in his mouth, and the wife had just begun to prepare their supper, when a gust of wind pushed open their cottage door. It set the windows to rattling and the dishes on the cupboard shelves to dancing.

"Husband," said the woman, "get up and close the door."

"I'll do no such thing," answered he. "I didn't open it. And I'll not close it. You close it yourself."

"I didn't open it either," said the wife. "And I'll certainly not close it."

"Very well," said the husband. "You didn't open it, and I didn't open it. But whichever of us speaks first from now on shall be the one to close the door."

To this silly remark the wife agreed. The wind whistled in and out of the cottage. The man sat stubbornly in his chair and shivered. And the wife had all she could do to keep her teeth from chattering as she went about making supper. But neither of these silly people would close the door.

Presently the woman placed on the table a large pat of yellow butter. She poured good rich cream into a low bowl. But she did not ask her husband to come to the table. So he just sat there.

A hungry pussycat wandered by. She looked in at the open door. The man did not throw his slippers at her and the woman did not seize the broom. So the cat came in. Neither the man nor the woman cried "Scat! Scat!"— so the cat jumped up on the table and soon her little pink tongue made short work of the butter and the cream. When she had finished, the cat jumped down to the floor and began to wash herself from tail tip to ear tips. And still neither the man nor the woman said one word.

The woman then put on the table a platter of sizzling

neat patties. And again she did not ask her husband to
come and eat.

A large hungry dog came sniffing along. How good
the patties smelled! With one leap the dog was in the
cottage. Not the man, not the woman said a single word,

so the dog jumped up on the table and *gulp! gulp!—* there was an end to all the meat. Feeling very good, the dog licked his chops, jumped down to the floor, turned around and around and around and soon was fast alseep in a big furry ball. And still neither the man nor the woman said one word.

Then the woman put on the table a fresh cherry pie and a big pitcher of warm milk. And still she didn't ask her husband to come and eat.

A thief came along. He poked his head in at the open door. The man and the woman made no move. The thief stepped cautiously into the cottage. All remained quiet. The thief then sat down at the table and quicker than it takes to tell, he ate up the whole pie and drank all the milk. Then he gathered all the spoons and knives and forks together and put them into his pouch.

"These two must be deaf and dumb and blind," he said to himself. "Now, let's see. What else can I take?"

His eyes went around the room and soon spotted the woman's best china teapot.

"Now, there's something," he said aloud. "That should fetch me a pretty penny."

He went over to the cupboard and reached for the teapot. But at this the woman burst out at the top of her lungs:

"Vagabond! Rogue! Thief! Isn't it enough that you have eaten the whole pie and drunk all the milk and stolen all our silver? Must you have my best teapot too?"

Her cries so startled the cat and dog that both jumped to their feet, the cat hissing and spitting and the dog growling and barking. As for the thief, he was so astonished at all the sudden noise that he was frightened out of his wits. He dropped the teapot, clutched the silver tightly to him, and took to his heels. Out the open door he sped, with the cat and the dog in pursuit.

"After them, man!" cried the woman. "Will you sit there and do nothing while we lose everything?"

But the stubborn silly man, with all the food gone, the silver stolen, and the best teapot in a thousand pieces on the floor, only shrugged his shoulders and said:

"Wife, you spoke first. Now go and close the door."

The Princess Whom Nobody Could Silence

By P. C. Asbjornsen
Translated from the Norwegian
by H. L. Brækstad

There was once upon a time a king, and he had a daughter who would always have the last word. She was so perverse and contrary in her speech that no one could silence her. So the king therefore promised that he who would outwit her should have the princess in marriage and half the kingdom besides. There were plenty of those who wanted to try, I can assure you; for it isn't every day that a princess and half a kingdom are to be had.

The gate to the palace hardly ever stood still. The suitors came in swarms and flocks from east and west, both riding and walking. But there was no one who could silence the princess. At last the king announced that those who tried and did not succeed should be branded on both ears with a large iron; he would not have all this running about the palace for nothing.

So there were three brothers who had also heard about the princess, and as they were rather badly off at home, they thought they would try their luck and see if they could win the princess and half the kingdom. They were good friends and so they agreed to set out together.

When they had got a bit on the way, Ashiepattle found a dead magpie.

"I have found something! I have found something!" cried he.

"What have you found?" asked the brothers.

"I have found a dead magpie," said he.

"Faugh! Throw it away; what can you do with that?"

said the other two, who always believed they were the wisest.

"Oh, I've nothing else to do. I can easily carry it," said Ashiepattle.

When they had gone on a bit further Ashiepattle found an old willow-twig, which he picked up.

"I have found something! I have found something," he cried.

"What have you found now?" said the brothers.

"I have found a willow-twig," said he.

"Pooh! What are you going to do with that? Throw it away," said the two.

"I have nothing else to do, I can easily carry it with me," said Ashiepattle.

When they had gone still further he found a broken saucer and picked it up.

"Here, lads, I have found something! I have found something!" said he.

"Well, what have you found now?" said the brothers.

"A broken saucer," said he.

"Pshaw! Is it worth while dragging that along with you too? Throw it away!" said the brothers.

When they had gone a little bit further he found a crooked goat-horn and soon after he found a fellow to it.

"What have you found now?" said the brothers.

"Two goat-horns," answered Ashiepattle.

"Ugh! Throw them away! What are you going to do with them?" said they.

"Oh, I have nothing else to do. I can easily carry them with me," said Ashiepattle.

In a little while he found a wedge.

"I say, lads, I have found something! I have found something!" he cried.

"You are everlastingly finding something! What have you found now?" asked the two eldest.

"I have found a wedge," he answered.

"Oh, throw it away! What are you going to do with it?" said they.

"Oh, I have nothing else to do. I can easily carry it with me," said Ashiepattle.

As he went along the king's fields, which had been freshly manured, he stooped down and took up an old boot-sole.

"Hullo, lads! I have found something! I have found something!" said he.

"Heaven grant you may find a little sense before you get to the palace!" said the two. "What is it you have found now?"

"An old boot-sole," said he.

"Is that anything worth picking up? Throw it away! What are you going to do with it?" said the brothers.

"Oh, I have nothing else to do. I can easily carry it with me, and—who knows?—it may help me to win the princess and half the kingdom," said Ashiepattle.

"Yes, you look a likely one, don't you?" said the other two.

So they went in to the princess, the eldest first.

"Good day," said he.

"Good day to you!" answered she, with a shrug.

"It's terribly hot here," said he.

"It's hotter in the fire," said the princess. The branding iron was lying waiting in the fire. When he saw this he was struck speechless, and so it was all over with him.

The second brother fared no better.

"Good day," said he.

"Good day to you," said she, with a wriggle.

"It's terribly hot here," said he.

"It's hotter in the fire," said she.

With that he lost both speech and wits, and so the iron had to be brought out.

Then came Ashiepattle's turn.

"Good day," said he.

"Good day to you," said she, with a shrug and a wriggle.

"It is very nice and warm here," said Ashiepattle.

"It's warmer in the fire," she answered. She was in no better humor now she saw the third suitor.

"Then there's a chance for me to roast my magpie on it," said he, bringing it out.

"I'm afraid it will sputter," said the princess.

"No fear of that! I'll tie this willow-twig round it," said the lad.

"You can't tie it tight enough," said she.

"Then I'll drive in a wedge," said the lad, and brought out the wedge.

"The fat will be running off it," said the princess.

"Then I'll hold this under it," said the lad, and showed her the broken saucer.

"You are so crooked in your speech," said the princess.

"No, I am not crooked," answered the lad, "but this is crooked," and he brought out one of the goat-horns.

"Well, I've never seen the like!" said the princess.

"Here you see the like," said he, and brought out the other horn.

"It seems you have come here to wear out mv soul!" she said.

"No, I have not come here to wear out your soul, for I have one here which is already worn out," answered the lad, and brought out the old boot-sole.

The princess was so dumbfounded at this, that she was completely silenced.

"Now you are mine!" said Ashiepattle, and so he got her and half the kingdom into the bargain.